The Official

Freebies

for
Kids

STICKERS, GAMES, BOOKS, AND TOYS—
ALL FOR NEXT TO NOTHING

By the Editors of *Freebies* Magazine

Illustrations by Catherine Leary

Lowell House Juvenile
Los Angeles

Contemporary Books
Chicago

Acknowledgments

It is difficult to put together a book of this nature without the help of talented and dedicated people working together. The staff at FREEBIES has a special thanks for the commitment of RGA/Lowell House to this project. Their support made it happen.

Special thanks are reserved for Abigail Koehring, Margaret Koike, Don Weiner, and Linda Cook for the research, writing, and coordination of the material in this book.

Special mention must also be given to Lisa Melton, Amy Hanson, Peter Hoffman, and the rest of the crew at RGA/Lowell House for the editing, the design, and the final push to complete the project.

Text Design: Brenda Leach/Once Upon a Design

Manufactured in the United States of America
ISBN: 1-56565-044-1
Registered with the Library of Congress

10 9 8 7 6 5 4 3

Contents

About This Book

The Official Freebies for Kids contains more than 130 freebie offers that you can get through the mail. The FREEBIES editors reviewed hundreds of offers before making the selections for this book. Each freebie is described as accurately as possible.

How to Use This Book

1. Follow the directions. Each offer specifies how to order the freebie. Some offers may ask for a SASE (a long Self-Addressed, Stamped Envelope). If a small postage or handling fee is requested, include the proper amount (a check or money order is usually preferred). Some suppliers may wait for out-of-town checks to clear before honoring requests. If you are sending coins, be sure to use a single piece of tape to tape them down.

2. Print all information. Not everyone's handwriting is easy to read, so *neatly* print your name, address, and the complete spelling of your city on your request. Be sure to include your return address on the outside of your mailing envelope. Use a ballpoint pen when you write, because pencils can often smear, and felt-tip or ink pens easily smudge.

3. Allow time for your request to be processed and sent. Some suppliers send their offers by first-class mail. Others use bulk-rate mail, which can take up to eight weeks. Suppliers get thousands of requests each year and may process them slowly or right away, depending on the time of the year.

4. **What to do if you are unhappy with your freebie product.** If you are unhappy or have complaints about an offer, or if you have not received your offer within eight to ten weeks of your request, let FREEBIES know. Although the FREEBIES editors do not stock the items or offer refunds from their offices, they can follow up on your complaints with any supplier. Suppliers that generate too many complaints will not be included in future editions. Send your complaints, comments, or suggestions to:

FREEBIES Book Editors
1135 Eugenia Place
Carpinteria, CA 93013

5. **And there is more!** If you like the freebie offers in this book and want to find out about more great freebies, then you should subscribe to *FREEBIES Magazine*. For only $5.00 a year (to the readers of this book), FREEBIES sends you five great issues, each filled with more than 100 freebies. See the special offer on page 79.

Get a free copy of **Model Railroading Magazine** before the train whistle blows! It's filled with information about the exciting hobby of model railroading.

You will also receive a copy of **Discovering Miniatures Magazine**. It is jam-packed with photographs and information about the fascinating world of miniatures.

Send: Your name & address

Ask For: *Model Railroading Magazine*
& Discovering Miniatures Magazine

Mail To: Kalmbach Publishing
Marketing Dept.
21027 Crossroads Circle
Waukesha, WI 53187

If you enjoy collecting stamps, then you'll love this unique **coloring book & Hungarian postage stamps set** that is enjoyed by children in Hungary.

COLORING BOOK & STAMPS

POSTAL PLUS

Learn all about Hungary as you match each of the 24 Hungarian stamps to its picture in the 8½" x 11" coloring book. Then, color away!

Send: $2.00 postage & handling

Ask For: Coloring book & Hungarian postage stamps set

Mail To: JOLIE
P.O. Box 20
Roslyn Heights, NY 11577-0144

EDUCATIONAL BROCHURE

Reach for the Stars

Do you like math and science? Do you like stars? You may want to consider a career as an astronomer. Astronomy is the study of the stars and is the world's oldest science. You can learn more about careers in this field if you send for the 24-page **brochure** titled *Understanding the Universe: A Career in Astronomy.* The brochure explains what astronomers do and how you can prepare yourself for a career as an astronomer. The publication also lists schools that offer advanced programs in astronomy.

Send: 50¢ postage & handling

Ask For: *Understanding the Universe: A Career in Astronomy*

Mail To: AAS Education Office
University of Texas
Dept. of Astronomy, RLM 15.308
Austin, TX 78712-1083

Start your own herb garden with this package of five different **herb seeds**.

You'll receive Italian basil, sage, French sorrel, parsley, and bouquet dill seeds in a set.

Send: $1.00 postage & handling

Ask For: Herb seeds package

Mail To: Clyde Robin Herbs
P.O. Box 57043
Hayward, CA 94545

HERB SEEDS

THE SPICE OF LIFE

Calling all video game buffs! Put down your joysticks and grab your pens! Play It Again, the world's largest dealer of

used video game cartridges, will send you a **catalog** along with an **information booklet** that tells you how to buy and sell used systems and games from Nintendo, Super Nintendo, Sega Genesis, Game Boy, and Turbographix-16 (all IBM-compatible).

Send: $1.00 postage & handling

Ask For: Catalog & information booklet on buying & selling used video games

Mail To: Play It Again
P.O. Box 6718-F
Flushing, NY 11365

You will certainly want to count the **pennies** in this collection of **Lincoln-head pennies!**

Each of the 14 pennies is over 50 years old and features the "wheat design" back instead of the current Lincoln Memorial design. Remember, a penny saved is a penny earned—especially one from this bunch!

Send: $2.00 postage & handling

Ask For: Lincoln-head pennies

Mail To: Joan Alexander
P.O. Box 213
Roslyn Heights, NY 11576-0213

Postcards do a lot more than just remind you of the places you've been. You can learn all sorts of interesting things about history, art, architecture, geography, and many other subjects through postcard collecting.

Start your own collection with this **beginner's postcard kit & information sheet**. You will receive five postcards from different eras and places. The information sheet helps you figure out when and how the cards were printed.

POSTCARD KIT
Postcard Passion

Send:	$1.50 postage & handling
Ask For:	Beginner postcard kit & information sheet
Mail To:	Joan Nykorchuk
	13236 N. 7th Street, #4
	Suite 237
	Phoenix, AZ 85022

NATURE STAMPS

NATURAL BEAUTY

No matter what your favorite season is, you'll love this wonderful collection of **nature postage stamps.**

The packet contains 100 colorful stamps from around the world. Let your eyes do the walking through this collection, and you can see the beautiful, faraway places that you've dreamed about!

Send:	$1.00 postage & handling
Ask For:	Nature postage stamps
Mail To:	Nature Stamps
	P.O. Box 466
	Port Washington, NY 11050

CATALOG & RUBBER STAMP

STAMP OF APPROVAL

This is one offer you won't want to miss. **The Rubberstampler Catalog** has a splendid array of rubber stamps that you can order.

The hefty, 48-page catalog also comes with a $1.00 refund **coupon** and a miniature **rubber stamp** that you can mount on a piece of wood or plastic.

Send: $2.00 postage & handling

Ask For: *The Rubberstampler Catalog*, coupon, and rubber stamp

Mail To: Rubberstampler—FB
1945 Wealthy, SE
Grand Rapids, MI 49506-2919

Have you dreamed of driving to victory in a soapbox derby racer that you built yourself? Then request this thorough **All-American Soapbox Derby** book and learn how you can compete in exciting derbies on the local and national levels.

The 22-page book includes photos of the race winners and the cars they constructed. So, racers, start your engines!

BOOK

Derby Dreams

Send: Your name & address

Ask For: *All-American Soapbox Derby* book

Mail To: All-American Soapbox Derby
P.O. Box 7233
Akron, OH 44306

STAMP CATALOG

Stamps Galore

How do you get some of the most unusual postage stamps from around the world sent to your house? Send for the **stamps on approval catalog.**

This catalog offers bargains on stamps from the United States, Canada, and the United Nations. You can also order albums, accessories, and sports cards.

Send: Your name & address

Ask For: Stamps on approval catalog

Mail To: Jamestown Stamp Company, Inc.
341 E. 3rd Street
Jamestown, NY 14701-0019

Make your own unique designs with this **rubber stamp** offer.

The supplier will try to fill your special request (look below for a few ideas to choose from). You will also receive a **sheet of creative stamping ideas**, a **catalog** of additional designs, and a $1.00 discount **coupon** toward any order.

Send: $1.00 postage & handling

Ask For: Rubber stamp (specify a design: holiday, favorite animal, hobby, or other interest), sheet of stamping ideas, and catalog

Mail To: Something for Everyone
P.O. Box 711
Woodland Hills, CA 91365

RUBBER STAMP

ONE OF A KIND

¡Hola! Begin to learn Spanish and follow an authentic Latin American recipe by reading this free issue of the Spanish lesson newsletter **Bueno.**

The eight-page quarterly publication makes learning Spanish a snap. It teaches words in both English and Spanish and includes phonetic spellings of Spanish words.

SPANISH LESSON

Se Habla Español

> **Send:** A long SASE
>
> **Ask For:** *Bueno* Spanish lesson newsletter
>
> **Mail To:** Lesson
> Dept. FM
> 29481 Manzanita Drive
> Campo, CA 91906

POSTAGE STAMPS

POSTAL PLEASURES

History is at your fingertips—captured in postage stamps! Begin your own private collection by ordering this **assortment of old postage stamps.**

This group of 25 stamps includes six Disney theme stamps from around the world. In addition, the array contains a U.S. 2¢ Columbian Exposition stamp dated 1892.

> **Send:** $2.00 postage & handling
>
> **Ask For:** Assortment of postage stamps
>
> **Mail To:** Bick International
> Dept. FB
> P.O. Box 917
> Van Nuys, CA 91408

Find the perfect kite, flying toy, wind sock, or boomerang for your abilities and interests. Request the full-color, fascinating **Into the Wind catalog** and celebrate the wind!

The outstanding 80-page catalog will also captivate adults who are serious kite flyers and kite builders.

CATALOG

GO FLY A KITE

Send:	Your name & address
Ask For:	Into the Wind catalog
Mail To:	Into the Wind 1408 Pearl Street Boulder, CO 80302

COMMEMORATIVE STAMPS
Super Stamps

If you want to add some unusual postage stamps to your growing collection, send for this set of canceled commemorative **U.S. stamps.**

The unique set includes 100 stamps that are no longer in circulation. Some of them date as far back as World War II. Others honor such great Americans as football coach Knute Rockne and poet Marianne Moore.

Send:	$2.00 postage & handling
Ask For:	Canceled commemorative stamps
Mail To:	Joan Alexander P.O. Box 7 Roslyn, NY 11576

Super Sports Stuff

Most professional sports franchises offer free materials, such as season schedules and ticket information, to their enthusiastic fans. Some teams even give away fan packages that may contain stickers, photos, fan club info, catalogs, and more.

To get these great gifts, all you need to do is write the name of your favorite team on your request card and ask for a "fan package." We've compiled the addresses of all the professional basketball and football teams. Although not all teams require it, we recommend you send a SASE to help process your request.

Here's another tip: If you want to contact a specific player on your favorite team, address the envelope to his attention. Keep in mind that because of the high volume of fan mail each team receives, it may take more than eight weeks to get a response. So, be a good sport!

NATIONAL BASKETBALL ASSOCIATION

Atlanta Hawks
1 CNN Center
South Tower, Suite 405
Atlanta, GA 30303

Boston Celtics
151 Merrimac St., 5th Fl.
Boston, MA 02114

Charlotte Hornets
Fan Mail
Hive Dr.
Charlotte, NC 28217

Chicago Bulls
980 N. Michigan Ave.,
Suite 1600
Chicago, IL 60611-4501

Cleveland Cavaliers
Community Relations
2923 Streetsboro Rd.
Richfield, OH 44286

Dallas Mavericks
Reunion Arena
777 Sports St.
Dallas, TX 75207

Denver Nuggets
1635 Clay St.
Denver, CO 80204

Detroit Pistons
2 Championship Dr.
Auburn Hills, MI 48326

Golden State Warriors
Oakland Coliseum Arena
Oakland, CA 94621-1995

Houston Rockets
P.O. Box 272349
Houston, TX 77277

Indiana Pacers
300 E. Market St.
Indianapolis, IN 46204

Los Angeles Clippers
L.A. Memorial Sports Arena
3939 S. Figueroa
Los Angeles, CA 90037

Los Angeles Lakers
Great Western Forum
P.O. Box 10
Inglewood, CA 90306

Miami Heat
Miami Arena
Miami, FL 33136-4102

Milwaukee Bucks
1001 N. 4th St.
Milwaukee, WI 53203

Minnesota Timberwolves
600 1st Ave. North
Minneapolis, MN 55403

New Jersey Nets
Brendan Byrne Arena
East Rutherford, NJ 07073

New York Knicks
Madison Square Garden
4 Penn Plaza
New York, NY 10001

Orlando Magic
1 Magic Pl.
Orlando Arena
Orlando, FL 32801

Philadelphia '76ers
Veteran Stadium
P.O. Box 25040
Philadelphia, PA 19147

Phoenix Suns
P.O. Box 1369
Phoenix, AZ 85001

Portland Trail Blazers
Lloyd Bldg., Suite 950
700 NE Multnomah St.
Portland, OR 97232

Sacramento Kings
1 Sports Parkway
Sacramento, CA 95834

San Antonio Spurs
600 E. Market St., Suite 102
San Antonio, TX 78205

Seattle Supersonics
C-Box 900911
Seattle, WA 98109

Utah Jazz
301 W. South Temple
Salt Lake City, UT 84101

Washington Bullets
Capital Centre
Landover, MD 20785

AMERICAN CONFERENCE FOOTBALL TEAMS

Buffalo Bills
1 Bills Dr.
Orchard Park, NY 14127

Cincinnati Bengals
200 Riverfront Stadium
Cincinnati, OH 45202

Cleveland Browns
Cleveland Stadium
Cleveland, OH 44114

Denver Broncos
13655 E. Dove Valley Pkwy.
Englewood, CO 80112

Houston Oilers
6910 Fannin St.
Houston, TX 77030

Indianapolis Colts
7001 W. 56th St.
Indianapolis, IN 46224

Kansas City Chiefs
1 Arrowhead Dr.
Kansas City, MO 64129

Los Angeles Raiders
332 Center St.
El Segundo, CA 90245

Miami Dolphins
Joe Robbie Stadium
2269 NW 199th St.
Miami, FL 33056

New England Patriots
Foxboro Stadium - Route 1
Foxboro, MA 02035

New York Jets
100 Fulton Ave.
Hempstead, NY 11550

Pittsburgh Steelers
Three Rivers Stadium
300 Stadium Cir.
Pittsburgh, PA 15212

San Diego Chargers
Jack Murphy Stadium
9449 Friars Rd.
San Diego, CA 92108

Seattle Seahawks
11220 NE 53rd St.
Kirkland, WA 98033

NATIONAL CONFERENCE FOOTBALL TEAMS

Atlanta Falcons
Suwanee Rd. at I-85
Suwanee, GA 30174

Chicago Bears
Halas Hall
250 N. Washington Rd.
Lake Forest, IL 60045

Dallas Cowboys
Cowboys Center
1 Cowboys Pkwy.
Irving, TX 75063-4727

Detroit Lions
1200 Featherstone Rd.
Pontiac, MI 48057

Green Bay Packers
1265 Lombardi Ave.
Green Bay, WI 54304

Los Angeles Rams
2327 W. Lincoln Ave.
Anaheim, CA 92801

Minnesota Vikings
9520 Viking Dr.
Eden Prairie, MN 55344

New Orleans Saints
1500 Poydras St.
New Orleans, LA 70003

New York Giants
Giants Stadium
East Rutherford, NJ 07073

Philadelphia Eagles
Broad St. & Pattison Ave.
Philadelphia, PA 19148

Phoenix Cardinals
P.O. Box 888
Phoenix, AZ 85001-0888

San Francisco 49ers
4949 Centennial Blvd.
Santa Clara, CA 95054

Tampa Bay Buccaneers
1 Buccaneer Pl.
Tampa, FL 33607

Washington Redskins
P.O. Box 17247
Dulles International Airport
Washington, DC 20041

AMERICAN LEAGUE BASEBALL TEAMS

Baltimore Orioles
Memorial Stadium
Baltimore, MD 21218

Boston Red Sox
4 Yawkey Way
Boston, MA 02115

California Angels
P.O. Box 2000
Anaheim, CA 92803

Chicago White Sox
333 W. 35th St.
Chicago, IL 60616

Cleveland Indians
Cleveland Stadium
Cleveland, OH 44114

Detroit Tigers
Public Relations
2121 Trumbull Ave.
Detroit, MI 48216

Kansas City Royals
P.O. Box 419969
Kansas City, MO 64141

Milwaukee Brewers
201 S. 46th St.
Milwaukee, WI 53214

Minnesota Twins
501 Chicago Ave. South
Minneapolis, MN 55415

New York Yankees
Yankee Stadium
Bronx, NY 10451

Oakland Athletics
Oakland Coliseum
Oakland, CA 94621

Seattle Mariners
P.O. Box 4100
Seattle, WA 98104

Texas Rangers
P.O. Box 90111
Arlington, TX 76010

Toronto Blue Jays
Sky Dome
300 Bremmer Blvd.,
Suite 3200
Toronto, Ontario, Canada
M5V 3B3
*Note: first-class postage to
Canada is 40¢*

NATIONAL LEAGUE BASEBALL TEAMS

Atlanta Braves
P.O. Box 4064
Atlanta, GA 30302

Chicago Cubs
Wrigley Field
1060 West Addison St.
Chicago, IL 60613

Cincinnati Reds
100 Riverfront Stadium
Cincinnati, OH 45202

Colorado Rockies
1700 Broadway, Suite 2100
Denver, CO 80290

Florida Marlins
100 NE 3rd Ave.
Ft. Lauderdale, FL 33301

Houston Astros
P.O. Box 288
Houston, TX 77001-0288

Los Angeles Dodgers
1000 Elysian Park Ave.
Los Angeles, CA 90012

Montreal Expos
P.O. Box 500, Station M
Montreal, Quebec, Canada
HIV 3P2
*Note: first-class postage to
Canada is 40¢*

New York Mets
Shea Stadium
Flushing, NY 11368

Philadelphia Phillies
Veteran Stadium
P.O. Box 7575
Philadelphia, PA 19101

Pittsburgh Pirates
Public Relations
P.O. Box 7000
Pittsburgh, PA 15212

St. Louis Cardinals
250 Stadium Plaza
St. Louis, MO 63102

San Diego Padres
P.O. Box 2000
San Diego, CA 92102

San Francisco Giants
Candlestick Park
San Francisco, CA 94124

SPORTS CARDS

It's a Hit

Are you a sports card collector? Then you'll want to grab this grab bag of **10 star & rookie sports cards**, featuring various players from recent years.

Sure to score big with baseball fans, the collection includes trading cards of such great athletes as Nolan Ryan, Cal Ripken, and Roger Clemens. You will receive cards of the supplier's choice, but if you have a special request, please include it.

Send: $1.50 postage & handling

Ask For: 10 star & rookie sports cards

Mail To: Star Cards
Rte. 2, P.O. Box 46B-1
Letart, WV 25263

Hey, all you collectors of sports memorabilia! Catch this high-scoring offer for **baseball series stickers**.

Each 7" x 7" card is loaded with eight different stickers, including the hat, uniform, and team logos for the featured baseball club. The choice of teams is up to the supplier, but you may include any special requests.

Send: $1.50 postage & handling for one card; $5.00 for four

Ask For: Baseball series stickers *(specify team)*

Mail To: NEETSTUF
Dept. MS-4
P.O. Box 459
Stone Harbor, NJ 08247

Do you know what the oldest organized sport in America is? Lacrosse! Find out the latest news, equipment, and training tips of this sport in this sample issue of **Lacrosse Magazine**. Both boys and girls play this challenging sport.

The 68-page publication is published by the Lacrosse Foundation.

Send: $2.00 postage & handling

Ask For: *Lacrosse Magazine* free issue

Mail To: Lacrosse Magazine
The Lacrosse Foundation
113 W. University Parkway
Baltimore, MD 21210

LACROSSE MAGAZINE

READ ALL ABOUT IT

We're sure this **Louisville Slugger®** **bat pen** or **bat key chain** will score high with you!

Each plastic 5" replica of a real Slugger bat is definitely a home-run hitter!

Send: $1.00 postage & handling for each

Ask For: Louisville Slugger® bat pen or bat key chain

Mail To: H & B Promotions
Dept. Freebies
P.O. Box 10
Jeffersonville, IN 47130

FAN MAGAZINE

YANKEE DOODLE DANDY

Put on your pinstripes and read all about one of New York's terrific baseball teams in this sample copy of **Yankees Magazine**.

This 84-page monthly magazine is a must-have for sports fans who want to know the latest player profiles, box scores, roster reviews, and farm team happenings.

Send: $2.00 postage & handling

Ask For: Sample copy of Yankees Magazine

Mail To: Yankees Magazine
Freebies Dept.
Yankee Stadium
Bronx, NY 10451

Kick off this season with the football fanatic's fantasy—a sample issue of **The Redskins Journal**.

The sports newspaper is dedicated to giving the latest play-by-plays of NFL Super Bowl champion, the Washington Redskins. Published 22 times a year, the 32-page journal will keep you up to date on stats, game summaries, and souvenir suppliers.

Send: $1.00 postage & handling

Ask For: Sample issue of *The Redskins Journal*

Mail To: Redskins Journal
P.O. Box 1062
Manassas, VA 22110

FISHING SUPPLIES CATALOG
GONE FISHING

Get out your fishing pole and extra big net because you're sure to catch some whoppers with the supplies featured in the **Twin Lakes Bait Company catalog**!

Dixie Dancer, Dixie Buzz Dancer, and Dixie Clicker Mini Buzz Bait are just a few of the lures that are featured in this free brochure. The next time you go fishing, don't tell your friends about the one that got away—use the tackle from this catalog and reel in a big one!

Send: A long SASE

Ask For: *Twin Lakes Bait Company* catalog

Mail To: Twin Lakes Bait Company
Dept. FM
P.O. Box 56
Rineyville, KY 40162

Cool & Creative Crafts

Send for this **three-dimensional 12-point star kit** and simply cut, fold, and glue your way into a galaxy of colorful stars! With this fun kit, you can decorate your bedroom ceiling, create great party decorations, and even make Christmas tree ornaments. The kit comes with instructions and enough paper to make two stars, each measuring 4" in diameter.

Send: $1.00 postage & handling

Ask For: Three-dimensional 12-point star kit

Mail To: Woolie Works—Star
6201 E. Huffman Road
Anchorage, AK 99516

What's so fun about this special teddy bear offer? You make it yourself!

Send for your own **teddy bear pattern & instructions** and make your own 6" teddy bear. Give this cuddly creature as a gift or add a hook to its back for a unique Christmas tree ornament. Either way, this bear will be extra-special because you made it!

Send: $1.00 postage & handling

Ask For: Teddy bear pattern & instructions

Mail To: Golden Fun Kits
P.O. Box 10697-FR
Golden, CO 80401

TEDDY
BEAR
PATTERN

READY
FOR
TEDDY

If you are bored with doing the same old things every day, send away for this creative **idea sheet**.

Included in this sheet is a recipe for Hobo bread and instructions for making washcloth slippers.

RECIPES & CRAFTS

Fun Projects

Send:	$1.25 postage & handling
Ask For:	Idea sheet
Mail To:	Generations
	117 11th Street
	Black Eagle, MT 59414

FRAME KIT

CHAIN OF MEMORIES

Your mom or dad probably remembers making zigzag paper chains from gum wrappers. Now you can create something similar but more sophisticated: You can request this **gum wrapper art kit** and weave a memorable photo frame from wallpaper strips.

The kit comes with a sheet of wallpaper plus complete instructions.

Send:	$1.00 postage & handling
Ask For:	Gum wrapper art kit
Mail To:	Alaska Craft
	Dept. GW/S
	P.O. Box 11-1102
	Anchorage, AK 99511

Do you own lots of little things but have nowhere to put them all? This easy-to-follow **heart-shaped basket pattern** will help you make one fantastic storage stuffer!

The pattern shows you how to make a cute 5" heart-shaped basket that is perfect for all kinds of small goodies—from earrings to hair clips. By using different fabrics, you can make several unique baskets to give away to friends or family. They'll love them!

FABRIC BASKET PATTERN

FULL OF HEART

Send: $1.00 postage & handling

Ask For: Heart-shaped basket pattern

Mail To: Bears and Babes
Dept. HB
P.O. Box 6062
Chillicothe, OH 45601

DOLL PATTERNS

Indian Dolls

If you love playing with dolls and collecting them, then this offer is just right for you. Send for these doll patterns that show you how to make your own Indian brave and Indian maiden without sewing!

The **two doll patterns** show you how to make cute 12" dolls using handkerchiefs and other household items.

Send: $2.00 postage & handling

Ask For: Indian brave & maiden doll patterns

Mail To: Southwest Savvy
P.O. Box 1361-FB
Apple Valley, CA 92307

Don't miss this opportunity to request these original **"Dinosaurus Fourus" wooden craft plans** to help you and a parent make fabulous puzzles, coin

WOOD CRAFT DESIGNS

DINO-MITE CRAFTS

banks, and clocks in the shapes of four different dinosaur species.

The set includes instructions for 12 different items that measure about 14" at the longest point. You will need a drill, scroll saw or bandsaw, pine stock, and plywood for this project.

Send: $2.00 postage & handling

Ask For: "Dinosaurus Fourus" wooden craft plans

Mail To: Southwest Savvy
P.O. Box 1361-DF
Apple Valley, CA 92307

RECYCLED SHOPPING BAGS

Recycle It!

Don't add more trash to our planet when you don't have to. Send away for these two **foolproof patterns** to recycle brown paper bags.

The patterns show you how to convert a brown paper bag into a purse or a handy fold-away bag. It's easy, fun, and good for the environment.

Send: $1.00 postage & handling

Ask For: Foolproof patterns

Mail To: Winslow Publishing
P.O. Box 38012-F
Toronto, ON, Canada M5N 3A8
(Note: first-class postage to Canada is 40¢)

Hot Invention

Here's a hot idea for a cool science fair project or a sizzling summer activity. It's a solar hot dog cooker that you can make from materials you have around the house.

Send for this four-page set of simple **instructions for making a sun-powered hot dog cooker** from cardboard and aluminum foil, and enjoy constructing your reflector-cooker and eating your sun-cooked dogs.

Send: A long SASE and 25¢

Ask For: Instruction manual for making a solar hot dog cooker

Mail To: Energy & Marine Center
P.O. Box 190
Port Richey, FL 34673

Are you head over heels for horses, but you can't have the real thing? Request these sensational **stick horse patterns**, and you can make your own!

RIDE 'EM COWBOY

With a few simple tools, supplies, and the easy-to-follow instructions, you and a parent can make three different stick horses. Before you know it, you'll be ready to giddyap!

Send: $1.25 postage & handling

Ask For: Stick horse patterns

Mail To: Peebles Western Patterns
Dupuyer Creek Road
P.O. Box 234
Dupuyer, MT 59432

HOWDY!

Your birds won't be scared by this miniature scarecrow. Ask for the **rubber-band scarecrow kit** to make a straw friend that you can set in your bedroom or in the backyard.

You will receive instructions, diagrams, and materials to make a 7" to 8" scarecrow. Simply shape, cut, and twist some twine and fabric, and you'll have one terrific autumn decoration.

Send: $1.00 postage & handling

Ask For: Rubber-band scarecrow kit

Mail To: Alaska Craft
Dept. SC/K
P.O. Box 11-1102
Anchorage, AK 99511

What can you do with all the beautiful shells you collect from the beach? Why not turn them into attractive pictures, jewelry, or chimes?

Send for *Sea Shell Designs*, a nine-page set of ideas and instructions for making all kinds of fun crafts out of your precious sea treasures.

Send: $1.25 postage & handling

Ask For: *Sea Shell Designs*

Mail To: Shellcraft
P.O. Box 2567
Bullhead City, AZ 86430

CRAFT
INSTRUCTIONS

SEA
SHELL
CRAFTS

Make some unique pinecone and papier-mâché critters with these **pinecone duck & owl patterns**.

The three instruction pages provide a materials list and diagrams for several different-size birds. You'll need to find your own pinecones!

> **Send:** $1.00 postage & handling
>
> **Ask For:** Pinecone duck & owl patterns
>
> **Mail To:** Pinecone Craft
> P.O. Box 2567
> Bullhead City, AZ 86430

> **PINECONE
> CRAFT
> IDEAS**
> ----------
>
> # FOWL
> # PALS

CLOTHING DYE IDEAS
Quick Change

Turn your old duds into a sensational new wardrobe with **Grade A Looks With Rit® Dye**.

This eight-page booklet shows you how to put together dye-namic outfits without spending big bucks. Dip your old jeans, T-shirts, and sweats in the dye baths included in this booklet, and watch them come alive!

> **Send:** Your name & address
>
> **Ask For:** *Grade A Looks With Rit® Dye*
>
> **Mail To:** Grade A Looks With Rit® Dye
> Dept. 231
> P.O. Box 307
> Coventry, CT 06238

Part of our American folk art heritage, whirligigs are delightful wind toys that are simple to construct and fun to watch.

Request this set of **instructions for Uncle Sam's whirligig,** and you'll be able to make a 17" plywood Uncle Sam with wind-driven spinning arms. The eight-page foldout includes a full-size pattern and a list of materials for this clever outdoor ornament.

Toy Instructions	
WACKY WHIRLIGIG	

Send: $1.00 postage & handling

Ask For: Instructions for Uncle Sam's whirligig

Mail To: Cherry Tree Toys, Inc.
P.O. Box 369-135 U.S.
Belmont, OH 43718

CRAFT INSTRUCTIONS

Paper Pals

Do you want to turn a simple piece of paper into a lovely bird? Learn the secrets of origami, the ancient Japanese art of paper folding, in the booklet **Easy Folded Paper Animals**.

The instruction booklet tells you how to make 12 different paper animals. Before long, you'll have your very own zoo!

Send: $2.00 postage & handling

Ask For: *Easy Folded Paper Animals*

Mail To: Winslow Publishing
550 Eglinton Avenue West
P.O. Box 38012-A
Toronto, ON, Canada M5N 3A8
(Note: First-class postage to Canada is 40¢)

Games 'n' Toys

Are you ready for a new twist to your old card games? This deck of **crooked playing cards** is sure to add an interesting curve on "Go Fish"!

Each of these oddball cards is shaped like an S, but like a normal deck, this wacky set contains all the correct cards and suits.

Send: $2.00 postage & handling

Ask For: Crooked playing cards

Mail To: NEETSTUF
Dept. F-15
P.O. Box 459
Stone Harbor, NJ 08247

Try your hand at a free, autographed **Brain Baffler** puzzle and see how fast you can find the hidden words and arrange the leftover letters. Created by 20-year-old Jodi Jill, one of the youngest syndicated newspaper columnists in America, this puzzle has stumped some of the cleverest minds.

Send: A long SASE

Ask For: Brain Baffler puzzle

Mail To: Free Puzzle
Attn. Jodi Jill
2888 Bluff Sreet, Suite 143
Boulder, CO 80301

"A my name is Alice, my husband's name is Al, we came from Alabama and we sell Apples" is only one of the fun jump rope favorites you'll find in the book **Jump Rope Rhymes**.

This pocket-sized, 32-page book includes 28 rhymes created just for jump roping. So jump on this offer right away!

Send: $1.00 postage & handling
plus a SASE with TWO first-class stamps

Ask For: Jump Rope Rhymes

Mail To: Jump Rope Rhymes
Practical Parenting
18326 Minnetonka Boulevard
Deephaven, MN 55391

GLIDERS

PREHISTORIC PAN AM

Paper airplanes are fun to fly, but you just can't beat this Pterosaur dinosaur glider, unless of course, you have the piper tri-pacer and eagle-hawk **gliders.**

Made of Styrofoam, each glider comes in several easy-to-assemble pieces. Place the flight weight on the front, and the finished plane will glide just about anywhere.

Send: $1.00 postage & handling

Ask For: Pterosaur dinosaur, piper tri-pacer, or eagle-hawk glider

Mail To: Peggy's Stuff
P.O. Box 274
Avon, MA 02322-0274

If you're looking for a creative, fun gift, then these gigantic, plastic **inflatable toys** are for you!

You can choose from a **crayon** that's 4 feet tall, a **dolphin** that's almost 3 feet from nose to tail, and a **dinosaur** that's almost 3 feet long. The portable, inflatable toys can also liven up your bedroom decor.

INFLATABLE TOY

Big Blow-ups

Send:	$2.25 postage & handling (crayon) $2.00 postage & handling (dolphin) $2.50 postage & handling (dinosaur)
Ask For:	Crayon, dolphin, or dinosaur
Mail To:	Mr. Rainbows P.O. Box 387 Dept. F2-38 (crayon) /Dept. F2-39 (dolphin) /Dept. F2-40 (dinosaur) Avalon, NJ 08202

TRICK NICKEL

HEADS OR TAILS?

This **trick nickel** will astound your friends and family, who won't be able to beat the odds.

Choose either a two-headed or two-tailed nickel, and you'll also receive a novelty **catalog** and a $2 **coupon**. This trick will double your pleasure!

Send:	$2.00 postage & handling for one; $3.00 for two
Ask For:	Trick nickel (specify two-headed or two-tailed nickel)
Mail To:	Showplace Novelty & Magic Coin Dept. Crossroads Plaza #92 Salt Lake City, UT 84144

Send for **Let's Solve the Smokeword Puzzle,** and you'll go bonkers trying to solve this challenging brainteaser.

Produced by the American Lung Association, this mind boggler uses smart no-smoking slogans in this tough crossword puzzle.

Send:	Your name & address
Ask For:	Let's Solve the Smokeword Puzzle
Mail To:	American Lung Association P.O. Box 596-FB #0071 New York, NY 10116-0596

WORD PUZZLE

Crossword Smarts

GAME WATCHES

TICK-TOCK!

Time doesn't stand still, so you'd better order these snazzy **puzzle watches** before it's too late!

You will receive four plastic toy timepieces with this offer. Each colorful play watch contains a tiny pinball game that will make the hours fly by!

Send:	$1.30 postage & handling
Ask For:	Puzzle watches
Mail To:	The Complete Traveler 490 Route 46 East Fairfield, NJ 07004

This humdinger of an offer will have you playing a **full-size harmonica** in no time!

This resonant, 5" mouth harp has 32 holes. You can make up your own fun tunes or accompany your favorite songs on the radio with this delightful musical instrument.

> **Send:** $2.00 postage & handling
>
> **Ask For:** Full-size harmonica
>
> **Mail To:** Christian Treasures
> P.O. Box 1112
> Huntington Beach, CA 92647

MAGIC TRICK

ABRACADABRA

Amaze your friends and family with a magical mind-reading trick using these **mysterious cards of the veiled lady**.

This baffling set of six small cards enables even a beginning magician to perform this magnificent magic trick. Practice this trick once, and you'll be the hit of every party!

> **Send:** $1.25 postage & handling
>
> **Ask For:** Mysterious cards of the veiled lady
>
> **Mail To:** MailAway USA
> 635 N. Milpas Street
> Santa Barbara, CA 93103

This **picture frame key chain set** is the perfect place to keep important photos of your friends and family.

You will receive three plastic key chains that are shaped like a heart, a circle, and a square. They hold two photographs each and come in white with red, blue, or yellow stripes.

Send: $2.00 postage & handling

Ask For: Picture frame key chain set

Mail To: Mr. Rainbows
Dept. F2-45
P.O. Box 387
Avalon, NJ 08202

PICTURE FRAME KEY CHAINS

PICTURE

TOY DINOSAUR EGGS

Dinosaur Discoveries

Have you ever wondered what a dinosaur egg looks like when it's hatching? You don't have to imagine any more with this eggs-cellent offer for a pair of **toy dinosaur eggs**.

Each 1" egg contains an 8" sponge dinosaur that hatches when you place it in warm water. Eggs-traordinary!

Send: $1.50 postage & handling

Ask For: Pair of dinosaur eggs

Mail To: C & F Distributors
475 N. Broome Avenue
Lindenhurst, NY 11757

SCRATCH-OFF GAMES

SECRET SCRATCH-OFFS

You'll be itching to scratch off these great games! Send for a pack of three different **Scratchees™ games** to play with a pal when you're traveling or waiting at the dentist's office.

You will love uncovering the hidden symbols in such games as "Food Fight Frenzy" and "Mutant Parents from Planet Mars." The choice of games is up to the supplier.

Send: $1.00 postage & handling

Ask For: Three Scratchees™ games

Mail To: Decipher, Inc.
Freebies Scratchees Offer
P.O. Box 56
Norfolk, VA 23501-0056

Want to know where you can find the most outrageous, radically realistic reptile replicas? "Yes, I-guana know!"

With this offer you will receive one **rubber suction lizard** from an assortment of colorful and authentic-looking creatures. These scaly slitherers measure 3" long, not including their tails. Each has a suction cup that allows you to stick it to a window, refrigerator, or other smooth surface.

RUBBER SUCTION LIZARD

Leaping Lizards

Send: $1.25 postage & handling

Ask For: Rubber suction lizard

Mail To: Lightning Enterprises
P.O. Box 16121
West Palm Beach, FL 33416

This **clown doll** has a silly grin that is sure to put a smile on your face!

Sporting bright clown duds and vibrant yarn hair, this 7" doll has soft vinyl arms, legs, and head, and a stuffed fabric body. This perky pal wants to be your friend, so don't let him down!

Send:	$2.00 postage & handling
Ask For:	Clown doll
Mail To:	Christian Treasures
	P.O. Box 1112
	Huntington Beach, CA 92647

BALLOON HELICOPTER

HIGH-FLYING FUN

Up, up, and away! This **whistling balloon helicopter** is one high-flying toy.

The packet comes with three plastic wings, a small rotor, two balloons, and instructions to help you assemble your toy. Your helicopter will fly away whistling as it soars higher and higher in the sky.

Send:	$1.00 postage & handling
Ask For:	Whistling balloon helicopter
Mail To:	Whistling Balloon Helicopter
	P.O. Box 57043
	Hayward, CA 94545

What sounds like a video game and a telephone ring, AND keeps your keys together? An **Echo Killer eight-sound key chain!**

EIGHT-SOUND KEY CHAIN
A POCKETFUL OF SOUNDS

This unusual key chain plays various noises that sound like the real thing. Don't answer the phone just yet—it might be your key chain ringing!

Send: $2.00 postage & handling

Ask For: Echo Killer eight-sound key chain

Mail To: Eccor Wholesale
3710 Mendenhall S.
Memphis, TN 38115

RUBBER STAMPS
INSTANT ART

Even if you aren't an artist, you can make picture-perfect images of your favorite animal or hobby with these quality **rubber stamps**.

You will get two rubber stamps that you can create handles for by mounting them with rubber cement on bottle caps or small pieces of wood. Now grab an ink pad and stamp away!

Send: A long SASE with TWO first-class stamps

Ask For: Two rubber stamps
(specify your favorite animal or hobby)

Mail To: Ramastamps - K
7924 Soper Hill Road
Everett, WA 98205

Fright Fun

When Halloween rolls around, you'll want the scariest costume in town. To add the perfect touch to your ghoulish outfit, order the **Spifey Spider & Belfry Bat Pins.** The spider is fuzzy with two beady eyes and eight thin legs. The bat has a white face and two felt wings.

SPIDER & BAT PINS

Frightening Friends

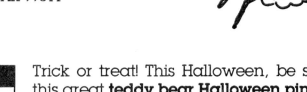

Send: $1.00 postage & handling

Ask For: Spifey Spider & Belfry Bat Pins

Mail To: Alaska Craft
Dept. SS/K
P.O. Box 11-1102
Anchorage, AK 99511

HALLOWEEN PIN

Halloween Teddy

Trick or treat! This Halloween, be sure to get this great **teddy bear Halloween pin.**

This miniature plush orange bear measures 2" in diameter and is surrounded by lace and orange beads. It can be fastened onto any festive outfit.

Send: $2.00 postage & handling for each

Limit: Four per address

Ask For: Teddy bear Halloween pin

Mail To: L. T. Hebbe
P.O. Box 337
Lanoka Harbor, NJ 08734

GHOST HAND PUPPET

Haunted Hand

Whether for Halloween or for a backyard puppet show, you will love this knitted white **ghost hand puppet** that resembles a friendly ghost.

The sturdy, 6" puppet will fit your hand like a glove and will provide plenty of fun.

Send: $2.00 postage & handling

Limit: Two per address

Ask For: Ghost hand puppet

Mail To: G. C. Hebbe
P.O. Box 337
Lanoka Harbor, NJ 08734

Ever wish that you could have a little friend to help you write your compositions and take your tests? With this offer you can have your own little **ghost writer** that clings to your pencil. The white 4" crocheted ghost has watchful black eyes and curls around a pencil. And, if you're lucky, it might scare your schoolwork away!

GHOST PENCIL TOPPER
Ghost Writer

Send: $1.00 for one; $1.75 for two

Ask For: Ghost writer pencil topper

Mail To: L. T. Hebbe
P.O. Box 337
Lanoka Harbor, NJ 08734

PUFFY STICKERS
STICKY SPOOKS

Add some Halloween horror to your locker or binder with these **puffy Halloween stickers**.

The set of eight 2" or 3" stickers includes both cute and scary Halloween characters in vivid colors. Pick a smiling scarecrow or a smirking skull, and show off your Halloween spirit!

Send: $1.50 postage & handling

Ask For: Puffy Halloween stickers

Mail To: McVehil's Mercantile
Road #8
P.O. Box 112-K
Washington, PA 15301

Need an accessory for your next Halloween costume that won't scare the socks off your teacher? Then send for these cute **pumpkin & black cat pins**.

PUMPKIN & BLACK CAT PINS
HALLOWEEN DESIGNS

The two pins are made of plastic canvas and yarn. The pumpkin face and black cat will show everyone that you wish them a Happy Halloween.

Send: $2.00 postage & handling (for both pins)

Limit: Four per address

Ask For: Pumpkin & black cat pins

Mail To: L. T. Hebbe
P.O. Box 337
Lanoka Harbor, NJ 08734

Did you know that Huckleberry Hound and Yogi Bear can tell fortunes? Just request these four nifty plastic Hanna-Barbera© cartoon character **fortune tellers** to help you discover your fortune.

FORTUNE TELLER

CLEAR AS CRYSTAL

Place the fortune teller in the palm of your hand. As it wiggles and twists, your fortune is revealed! The choice of characters is up to the supplier, but you may include a special preference.

> **Send:** $1.25 postage & handling
>
> **Ask For:** Fortune tellers
>
> **Mail To:** MailAway USA
> 635 N. Milpas Street
> Santa Barbara, CA 93103

HALLOWEEN DECALS

Trick or Treat!

Put one of these **Halloween decals** in your window, and scare away the tricksters!

These reusable plastic stick-ups show a frightening graveyard scene—complete with a hand rising up from the ground—or a red-eyed flying witch accompanied by bats. Measuring 8" high and 8" to 10" wide, each decal will stick to any window or mirror.

> **Send:** $1.50 postage & handling
>
> **Ask For:** Halloween decal (specify design: graveyard or witch)
>
> **Mail To:** McVehil's Mercantile
> Road #8
> P.O. Box 112-K
> Washington, PA 15301

Pet & Animal Pleasers

Do you love your cat more than anything? Then you'll want to send for this sample **catnip toy** and **brochure** of Dr. Daniels's catnip and health products. The kitten-size pillow is filled with 100% pure catnip. Your cat will thank you with its happy purrs.

Send: $2.00 postage & handling

Ask For: Catnip pillow & brochure

Mail To: Dr. A. C. Daniels, Inc.
109 Worcester Road
Webster, MA 01570

Have a new pet? This offer for the *You and Your Kitten* or *You and Your Puppy* **coloring book** will help show you how to take care of your new, cuddly friend.

Each fun 8½" x 11" coloring book includes games, illustrations, and instructions on handling a new pet.

Send: Your name & address

Ask For: Either *You and Your Kitten* or *You and Your Puppy* coloring book

Mail To: The ALPO Pet Center
P.O. Box 25200
Lehigh Valley, PA 18002-5200

ANIMAL ERASERS
Friendly Rubouts

Be kind to your mistakes! Rub them out with this nifty **bear** or **giraffe family eraser set.**

The pastel-colored set contains four erasers. The 1"- to 2"-long "mommy" eraser will help you get rid of big mistakes, while the three "baby" erasers help you wipe out smaller errors.

Send: $1.80 postage & handling

Ask For: Bear or giraffe family eraser set (specify bear or giraffe)

Mail To: Marlene Monroe
Dept. FA
6210 Ridge Manor Drive
Memphis, TN 38115-3411

Here are two fun animal faces that can stick your favorite drawings to the refrigerator and clip important schoolwork or fantastic photos at the same time. Request two **foam animal face magnetic clips** and start your own zoo!

Ranging from 2" to 3" in width and length, the magnetic clips feature vibrant, multicolored animal faces with goofy eyes. The selection of animals is up to the supplier, but you may include any special requests.

MAGNET
Two-In-One Fun

Send: $2.00 postage & handling

Ask For: Two foam animal face magnetic clips

Mail To: Marlene Monroe
Dept. FA
6210 Ridge Manor Drive
Memphis, TN 38115-3411

WHALE KIT

TAKE A WHALE TO SCHOOL

This **Whales of the World** kit has fun activities and all sorts of fascinating facts about these gentle giants of the sea.

The kit contains activity sheets, a glossary of terms, and a guide. It also includes information on how your school or class can adopt its very own whale through the nonprofit organization, The Whale Adoption Project. Wouldn't a whale be a great school mascot?

Send: $1.00 postage & handling

Ask For: *Whales of the World* teaching kit

Mail To: Whale Adoption Project
P.O. Box 388
North Falmouth, MA 02556

Stickers make fantastic seals on letters or decorations on packages. Purr-sonalize your correspondence with one of these **black & white cat stickers.**

Each of the eight stickers is 1¼" x 2" in size and features a beautiful feline in a unique pose.

Send: $1.00 postage & handling

Ask For: Eight black & white cat stickers

Mail To: Art Studio Workshops
Dept. 21
518 Schilling Circle NW
Forest Lake, MN 55025

Show off your pet with a unique **pet button!**

Send a photo of your faithful pet, and the supplier will turn it into a snazzy button. Measuring 2" in diameter, the badge can be attached to any cloth material.

> ```
> ------------------- PET BUTTON -------------------
> CUTE AS A BUTTON
> ```

Send:	$2.00 postage & handling, plus a small photo of your pet
Ask For:	Pet button
Mail To:	United Earth Friends®
	P.O. Box 51106
	Raleigh, NC 27609

Show how much you love cats with these fun **cat stamps.**

The sheet of 1½" x 2" stamps features colorful photographed cats in various poses. Each of the 40 stamps is also printed with a cute phrase that expresses your love for felines. They certainly rate a stamp of approval!

Send:	$2.00 postage & handling
Ask For:	Cat stamps
Mail To:	Pet Pride
	P.O. Box 1055
	Pacific Palisades, CA 90272

People aren't the only ones who need the vitamins that vegetables offer. Believe it or not, so do cats! Now you can order **seeds** that will help you grow your own edible grass for your favorite furry friend to eat.

EDIBLE GREENS

FELINE FIBER

You will receive enough seeds for two crops of grass. If your kitty doesn't get the fiber it needs, don't be surprised to see it chewing up the houseplants!

> **Send:** $2.00 plus first-class stamp
>
> **Ask For:** Edible greens seeds
>
> **Mail To:** Lake Country Nursery
> Route 2
> P.O. Box 1690
> Norridgewock, ME 04957

PET STICKERS

Decorative Decals

Personalize your notebooks, school locker, or lunch box with this collection of **shiny pet stickers.**

The three sheets of stickers feature colorful cats, dogs, and fish. Each sticker has a metallic sheen that makes them sparkle.

> **Send:** $2.00 postage & handling
>
> **Ask For:** Shiny pet stickers
>
> **Mail To:** Mr. Rainbows
> Dept. F2-1
> P.O. Box 387
> Avalon, NJ 08202

Do you love to spoil your cat? Order two colorful booklets on **Make Your Own Cat Toys,** and learn how to make 11 adorable kitty playthings. These handy guides also offer alternatives for cats who do not like catnip. In addition, your feline pet will receive a **free cat toy!**

Send: $2.00 postage & handling

Ask For: *Make Your Own Cat Toys* and free cat toy

Mail To: AKI KAO KITTY CACHE
1515 S. Clermont Street
Denver, CO 80222-3805

Tell everyone how you feel about your frisky friends by proudly wearing an **animal lovers button.**

> **PET BUTTONS**
> **A LITTLE LOVE**

The colorful buttons come in various cartoon designs with such cute phrases as "Love Me, Love My Cat," "Pets need T.L.C.," and "I Love Animals." You may request a certain button or let the supplier surprise you.

Send: $1.50 postage & handling

Ask For: Animal lovers button

Mail To: Bella Buttons
P.O. Box 1953
South Bend, IN 46634-1953

Lions and tigers and bears, oh my! This **zoo notepad** will liven up any notes you may have to take.

The 4¼" x 5½" zoo notepad has 50 sheets and is printed in black on white with an elephant or lion design. Through this offer, you can request a set of six different pads, including bear, turtle, monkey, and giraffe designs.

Send: $1.50 for one; $6.75 for six

Ask For: Zoo notepad   (specify design: elephant or lion or all six)

Mail To: Gingerbread House
11216 N. 500 East
Ossian, IN 46777

Is your kitty tired of the same toys? This super **catnip bonbon** is sure to liven up any cat's day.

Your feline friend will love playing keep-away with this kitty toy made of organic catnip wrapped in colorful cloth. Your order also includes a copy of **Blythe Designs Cat-a-log.**

CATNIP BONBON

CRAZY CAT TOY

Send: $1.00 for one; $5.00 for six

Ask For: Catnip bonbon

Mail To: Blythe Designs
P.O. Box 1750-F
Seattle, WA 98107

Rats have been given a bad rap! Get the record straight and learn about these friendly critters in a sample issue of **The Rat Report,** an informative publication created by the "big cheese" of a state university rat lab.

This interesting newsletter explains the benefits of having rats as pets and answers questions about choosing, training, and caring for these intelligent, clean rodents.

Send:	A long SASE
Ask For:	Sample issue of *The Rat Report* newsletter
Mail To:	PET-ABLES 1010½ Broadway Chico, CA 95928

Meow! Cat lovers will go bonkers over these **wooden cat cutouts.**

The package includes painting instructions, along with two small wooden kitten cutouts and their larger mother.

CAT CRAFT
Purrfect Pals

Send:	$2.00 postage & handling
Ask For:	Playful kittens & their momma
Mail To:	Chapman's Woodcraft HC-30 P.O. Box 340 Mesilla Park, NM 88047

Your kitty will be jealous when you keep your keys on this **catnip key chain/cat toy.**

CATNIP KEY CHAIN

CAT-CHY KEY CHAIN

Shaped like a cat's face, with felt ears and thread whiskers, these fabric toys are filled with catnip. If you want to make it a key chain, don't forget to ask for a key chain attachment.

Send: $2.00 postage & handling

Ask For: Catnip key chain/cat toy

Mail To: Janice Schade
Route 1
P.O. Box 21
Whitewater, WI 53190

PIERCED EARRINGS
Loop-de-Loop

Young ladies, lend me your ear—lobes! You won't be able to beat this steal of a deal for a pair of **14-karat layered gold hoop earrings.**

This glittering pair of pierced hoops has a twist design that will add a glamorous touch to any outfit.

Send: $1.50 postage & handling

Ask For: 14-karat layered gold hoop earrings

Mail To: KARAT Club
405 Tarrytown Road, Suite 215
White Plains, NY 10607

No matter how many colorful outfits you have in your closet, you're sure to find a terry cloth **ponytail holder** to match with this collection of two dozen different holders.

You will receive two packages covering the color spectrum from aqua blue to peach. These elastic holders will add a touch of style to any wardrobe.

Send: $2.00 postage & handling

Ask For: Ponytail holders

Mail To: Eccor Wholesale
3710 Mendenhall S.
Memphis, TN 38115

PONYTAIL HOLDERS
MIX AND MATCH

Are you afraid your gift will get lost in a big box? Then send for these **mini gift bags.**

GIFT CONTAINERS

ITTY BITTY BAGS

The five containers, made out of wallpaper samples, arrive flat and assemble easily. Measuring 1" x 2" x 3" (including handles), the containers are the perfect size for that small but special something.

Send: $1.00 postage & handling

Ask For: Five mini gift bags

Mail To: Alaska Craft
Dept. BG/S
P.O. Box 11-1102
Anchorage, AK 99511

RABBIT PONYTAIL HOLDERS

A Hare for the Hair

You don't have to wait for Easter to do your hair up with these **rabbit ponytail holders!**

Each of the two sets features two bunny ponytail holders. The rabbits are made of clear plastic and have colorful highlights on the ears. You'll want to wear them all year long!

Send: $2.00 postage & handling

Ask For: Two sets of plastic rabbit ponytail holders

Mail To: Eccor Wholesale
3710 Mendenhall S.
Memphis, TN 38115

Dress up your school and play clothes with a fun, stretchy 18" **Kids Pal necklace** that features colorful plastic beads and a matching painted wooden pendant. You can choose one of four styles: Halloween, Christmas, Easter, or "everyday," which is done in pastel colors.

> BEAD
> NECKLACE
> Fantastic
> Elastic

Send: $2.00 postage & handling per necklace

Limit: Three necklaces per address

Ask For: Kids Pal necklace
(specify style: Halloween, Christmas, Easter, or "everyday")

Mail To: Animal Pals Children's Jewelry
Dept. F
1598 St. Andrews Circle
Elgin, IL 60123

SNOWFLAKE STATIONERY

FROSTY GREETINGS

This winter, send your pen pals some cool greetings with this attractive **snowflake stationery.**

The stationery set comes with white envelopes, four sheets of heavy, pale blue, linenlike paper, and four white, die-cut snowflakes that you can glue anywhere on the paper.

Send: $1.00 postage & handling

Ask For: Snowflake stationery

Mail To: Alaska Craft
Dept. SN/S
P.O. Box 11-1102
Anchorage, AK 99511

Don't cry, it's not too late to take advantage of this **teardrop pendant & chain** offer!

The lovely teardrop pendant features a simulated pearl and hangs from an 18" layered gold chain. A sparkling addition to your jewelry collection, the necklace's cobra design will complement all of your favorite outfits.

Send:	$2.00 postage & handling
Ask For:	Teardrop pendant & chain
Mail To:	KARAT Club
	405 Tarrytown Road, Suite 215
	White Plains, NY 10607

TEARDROP NECKLACE

GLINT OF GOLD

CRAYON COMB & MIRROR SETS

Looking Good

You can look your best all day long with these handy **crayon comb & mirror sets.**

Shaped like giant crayons, these two compact sets each contain a comb and an accompanying mirror. They are the right size to tuck into a purse or book bag. Here's looking at you!

Send:	$1.50 postage & handling
Ask For:	Crayon comb & mirror sets
Mail To:	Mr. Rainbows
	Dept. F2-35
	P.O. Box 387
	Avalon, NJ 08202

This stunning **sterling silver charm** is definitely one "charming" offer you don't want to miss!

Choose from three lovely designs: two dainty ¼" silver hearts entwined, a ½" charm with the word "love" written in cursive, and a ¾" dollar sign charm. Through this offer, you can also order a sterling silver 7" bracelet to hang these sparkling charms on.

Send: $1.95 postage & handling for each charm or bracelet

Ask For: Sterling Silver Charm (specify design: entwined hearts, "Love," or dollar sign)

Mail To: Two Gals
P.O. Box 747
Forestville, CA 95436

Want to make some jazzy jewelry that tells the whole world who you are? Then send away for this neat do-it-yourself **alphabet bracelet kit.**

Each package comes with 40 alphabet beads, 36 colored beads, and an elastic band. There are enough supplies to make three bracelets, so you can mix and match the letters to spell out your friends' names, too!

Send: $2.00 postage & handling for three kits

Ask For: Three alphabet bracelet kits

Mail To: Who's Who Baby
8858 El Capitan
Fountain Valley, CA 92708

HEART-SHAPED ERASERS

From the Heart

Everyone makes mistakes, especially on classwork. And that's why these **heart-shaped fashion erasers** come in extra handy.

Each offer is good for two sets of erasers. If you're going to make a correction, do it in style!

Send: $1.50 postage & handling

Ask For: Heart-shaped fashion erasers

Mail To: Eccor Wholesale
3710 Mendenhall S.
Memphis, TN 38115

Awesome Books & Magazines

SAMPLE SCIENCE MAGAZINE

JUST THE FACTS

Explore the extraordinary world of science in this sample issue of **Science Weekly.**

This colorful four-page publication addresses one current science topic per issue. Each exciting issue has challenging exercises to test your science knowledge. Choose the reading level that's just right for you.

Send:	Your name & address
Limit:	One issue per address
Ask For:	*Science Weekly* (specify grade level: K through 8)
Mail To:	Science Weekly, Inc. Subscription Dept. P.O. Box 70154 Washington, DC 20088-0154

Sing your old favorites with the **Sing-Along Songs booklet.**

Filled with 38 familiar tunes such as "Oh! Susanna" and "Kookaburra," this wonderful booklet will help you change your tune!

SONG BOOKLET

Happy Hits

Send:	A long SASE plus $1.00 postage & handling
Ask For:	*Sing-Along Songs* booklet
Mail To:	Sing Along Songs Practical Parenting, Dept. KS-FRBE 18326 Minnetonka Boulevard Deephaven, MN 55391

Through this great offer, you can receive a sample copy of one of the following six magazines: **Turtle Magazine** (3 to 4 yrs.), **Humpty Dumpty** (4 to 5 yrs.), **Children's Playmate** (6 to 8 yrs.), **Jack & Jill** (7 to 10 yrs.), **Child Life** (9 to 11 yrs.), and **Children's Digest** (10 to 12 yrs.).

SAMPLE COPY OF
CHILDREN'S PUBLICATIONS
MAGAZINE MANIA

Send:	$1.25 each
Ask For:	(The magazine's title)
Mail To:	Children's Better Health Institute
	Attn: Jeanne Aydt, Sample "F"
	1100 Waterway Boulevard
	Indianapolis, IN 46206

You can make a difference in the world! Why not start with an issue of **KIND News?**

Published by the National Association for Humane and Environmental Education, the illustrated, four-page periodical promotes kindness to animals, people, and the environment. Choose the junior or the senior version.

Send:	A long SASE plus 50¢ postage & handling
Ask For:	*KIND News Jr.* (grades 2-4) or *KIND News Sr.* (grades 5-6)
Mail To:	KIND News
	Dept. FF
	67 Salem Road
	East Haddam, CT 06423-1736

If your tummy's grumbling for some chocolate, send for **Jeremyah's Chocolate Recipes for Kids,** an illustrated eight-page brochure that tells you how to make nine delicious desserts. Especially designed for you and a grown-up to bake together, some of the recipes in this book include Dinosaur Mud and Peanut Butter Chocolate Fudge.

CHOCOLATE RECIPES

JUST FOR KIDS

Send:	$1.25 postage & handling
Ask For:	*Jeremyah's Chocolate Recipes for Kids*
Mail To:	Jeremyah's Chocolate Recipes P.O. Box 7153 Loveland, CO 80537

PUBLICATION
Silent Speech

Pretend you're a mime and show how you feel without saying a word. That's just how deaf people express their emotions much of the time. Some people who have hearing loss use speech reading, sign language, finger spelling, and other forms of communication, as you'll learn in the illustrated booklet **How Deaf People Communicate.**

Written for kids just like you, this eight-page publication includes illustrations and diagrams of some of the most common signs for words.

Send:	$1.00 postage & handling
Ask For:	*How Deaf People Communicate*
Mail To:	National Info. Center on Deafness Freebies Offer/Gallaudet 800 Florida Avenue, NE Washington, DC 20002

You are what you eat! With this helpful brochure, **Guide to Good Eating,** learn how to eat the right foods for a healthy mind and body. The colorful, two-sided guide includes photographs and diagrams of the four food groups so that you can visualize balanced menus.

FOOD GUIDE

Be Good to Yourself

Send: A long SASE

Ask For: *Guide to Good Eating*

Mail To: National Dairy Council
O'Hare International Center
Dept. FL
10255 W. Higgins Road, Suite 900
Rosemont, IL 60018

COOKIE CUTTER & RECIPES

FOR COOKIE MONSTERS

"Be sorry for people, whoever they are, who live in a house where there's no cookie jar!" begins the charming **cookie recipe booklet** that accompanies the 3" polystyrene **cookie cutter** in this fantastic offer.

Send: $1.75 postage & handling

Ask For: Cookie recipe booklet & cookie cutter

Mail To: Gingerbread House
11216 N. 500 East
Ossian, IN 46777

HARMONICA BOOKLET
NEW NOTES

If you've always wanted to learn to play a tune on the harmonica, this is one offer you won't want to miss!

The **How to Play the Marine Band Type Hohner Harmonica** booklet is a simple 24-page guide for beginners. Follow the numbers and arrows in the booklet to learn to play popular, well-loved tunes.

Send: A long SASE

Ask For: *How to Play the Marine Band Type Hohner Harmonica*

Mail To: Dept. FD
Hohner, Inc.
P.O. Box 9375
Richmond, VA 23227

Chess, the king of board games, is enjoyed by both children and adults all over the world. Don't delay—learn how to play today!

You can learn the official rules of this fascinating strategy game with the pamphlet **Let's Play Chess.** **Let's Get Moving** is a special invitation for kids to join the U.S. Chess Federation and is also available through this offer.

PUBLICATION
Check-mate!

Send: A long SASE

Ask For: *Let's Play Chess* and *Let's Get Moving*

Mail To: Ms. Barbara A. DeMaro
U.S. Chess Federation
186 Route 9W
New Windsor, NY 12553

Calling all choco-holics! This offer for a pamphlet of **10 Chocolate Chunk Cookie recipes** and a **store coupon** will have you baking up a storm.

The delectable, naturally flavored, semisweet pieces of chocolate are perfect for all of the cookie recipes in this offer. Once you start baking, you'll be in cookie heaven!

Send: A long SASE

Ask For: Chocolate Chunk Cookie recipes & store coupon

Mail To: SACO Foods
Freebies Cookie Offer
P.O. Box 616
Middleton, WI 53562

Or call toll-free: 1-800-373-SACO

Want to hear the latest stories, jokes, mysteries, and current events on a cassette tape put together by kids just like you? Then send away for your issue of **BOOMERANG!,** the audio magazine.

This innovative 70-minute audiocassette makes short stories, world affairs, history, and other interesting topics come to life!

Send: $2.00 postage & handling

Ask For: *BOOMERANG!* free issue

Mail To: *BOOMERANG!* Magazine
123 Townsend Street, Suite 636-F
San Francisco, CA 94107

KIDS' AUDIO MAGAZINE

AWE- SOME AUDIO

Follow the adventures of Eric and Anna in South America's Chicma River Valley as they learn all about peanuts in **The Gold Peanut comic book.**

Published by the National Peanut Council, the 16-page comic book will surprise you with fascinating facts about the nut that's not really a nut!

Send: TWO first-class postage stamps

Ask For: *The Gold Peanut* comic book

Mail To: Peanuts
P.O. Box 1709
Rocky Mount, NC 27802-1709

Would you like to have fun items such as stickers, pencils, novelty erasers, magnets, sports stuff, sunglasses, stuff for mom and dad, and more?

Then you need *FREEBIES Magazine.* Each issue of *FREEBIES* features articles on approximately 100 fun items for the whole family that are available for free or for a small postage and handling cost (never more than $2).

Send: $2.00 postage & handling for a sample issue
or $5.00 for a one-year/5-issue subscription (regular rate is $8.95)

Ask For: Sample issue of *FREEBIES* or a one-year subscription as indicated above.

Mail To: *FREEBIES Magazine*
P.O. Box 5025
Dept. Kids
Carpenteria, CA 93014

If you like your meals sloppy and yummy, then **Sloppy Joe & the Gang Cookbook** is right up your alley.

RECIPE BOOK

MESSY FINGERS

This creative recipe book includes a number of variations on the classic burger. Learn how to make such tasty treats as Cheesy Joes, Pizza Joes, Cajun Joes, and even three vegetarian Joes. Watch out—you'll need lots of napkins for these!

> **Send:** $3.00 postage & handling
>
> **Ask For:** *Sloppy Joe & the Gang Cookbook*
>
> **Mail To:** The Source
> P.O. Box 81645
> Spring Valley, NV 89180

NUTRITION
FLYER

SNACK ATTACK

Don't eat those greasy chips anymore! Now you can satisfy the nibbler and snacker in you with the delicious, nutritious goodies in **Snacking: The Great American Pastime.**

Get your free copy of the six-panel flyer and munch your way to a healthier body!

> **Send:** Your name & address
>
> **Ask For:** *Snacking: The Great American Pastime*
>
> **Mail To:** Snacking: The Great American Pastime
> P.O. Box 1100
> Grand Rapids, MI 55745-1108

TRAVEL GAMES BOOK

Road Recreation

"Are we almost there yet?" You'll never ask that question again when you have this clever **Travel Games Family Fun Book.**

The 30-page road book includes several new games that involve scouting out signs, roofs, fences, and nature words and listening for specific types of sounds. The games are so entertaining that you may want to stay on the road even after you've reached your destination!

Send: $1.50 postage & handling

Ask For: *Travel Games Family Fun Book*

Mail To: The Beavers
HCR 70
P.O. Box 537
Laporte, MN 56461

Odds & Ends

This **stuffed teddy bear magnet** will keep your important papers from falling off the refrigerator.

The cute 3" bear magnet has plush beige fur and wears a red ribbon around its neck. There's no doubt about it, this little teddy has a "magnetic" personality!

MAGNET

BEAR BUDDY

Send: $2.00 postage & handling

Ask For: Stuffed teddy bear magnet

Mail To: Spring Valley Crafters
3421 Spring Valley Road
Newport, WA 99156

STICKERS

Sticker Savvy

Featuring phones, guitars, and drum sets, this offer for **stickers** will be music to your ears.

The decorative stickers come in colorful, metallic designs and can be used to personalize book bags or notebooks.

Send: $1.00 postage & handling

Ask For: Teen time telephone/rock 'n' roll stickers

Mail To: Mr. Rainbows
Dept. F2-51
P.O. Box 387
Avalon, NJ 08202

Down in the dumps? Turn a frown into a grin with the **happy face stickers**.

With 352 self-adhesive stickers, you certainly have more than enough to spread a little sunshine and share them with a friend!

> **Send:** $2.00 postage & handling
>
> **Ask For:** Happy face stickers
>
> **Mail To:** S. Brown
> P.O. Box 568
> Techny, IL 60082

You can show everybody who your favorite movie characters are with these great Mickey Mouse, *Addams Family*, and *101 Dalmatians* **buttons.**

Disney fans will want to wear the button of their favorite mouse or dalmatian, while fright fans should ask for the Addams Family badge that bears a photo of the film's cast. Each button has a white background and a pin backing that will attach to any cloth material.

> **Send:** $1.00 postage & handling for each one
>
> **Ask For:** Mickey Mouse, *Addams Family*, or *101 Dalmatians* button
>
> **Mail To:** Prairie Flower button offer
> P.O. Box 8664
> Riverside, CA 92515

Collect tiny treasures in these appealing **miniature glass bottles!** Perfect for small shells or little blossom buds, the four clear jars measure just 1½" tall and have white removable stoppers. You can also use them to hold safety pins, screws, paper clips, jewelry, or any small items that need a home.

BOTTLES

Junior Jars

> **Send:** $1.00 postage & handling
>
> **Ask For:** Four miniature glass bottles
>
> **Mail To:** Woolie Works Bottles
> 6201 E. Huffman Road
> Anchorage, AK 99516

MYLAR BALLOON

Balloon Buddies

Whether your favorite comic strip pet is Garfield or Snoopy, you won't want to pass up this offer for a **Garfield** or **Snoopy mylar balloon.**

The 9" mylar balloons depict the familiar cartoon faces of the feisty cat or lovable dog. To inflate, simply insert a straw in the heart-shaped balloon, blow it up, and seal it with tape or the heat of a curling iron. Now you've got a great balloon buddy!

> **Send:** A long SASE plus $1.00 postage & handling
>
> **Ask For:** Snoopy or Garfield mylar balloon
>
> **Mail To:** Mark-It
> Dept. F
> P.O. Box 246
> Dayton, OH 45405

NAME PLATES
WHAT'S IN A NAME?

Give your bedroom door or your teacher's desk a new look. Order these colorful **happy face name plates** and then everyone will know who's who!

You will receive four 3" x 10" name plates with this offer. Just fill in the appropriate name, fold along the scored lines, and stand or tape the plate wherever you want the name to be seen.

Send: $1.25 postage & handling

Ask For: Happy face name plates

Mail To: S. Brown
P.O. Box 568
Techny, IL 60082

You don't have to use that old cup to trace circles anymore! This terrific **tracing set** can help you draw pictures of your favorite theme, such as the zoo, farm, circus, holidays, or dinosaurs.

The plastic stencils measure 2½" to 3" long and come in a variety of colors. Each tracing set comes with stencils of appropriate objects.

Send: 75¢ postage & handling

Ask For: Tracing set (specify theme: zoo, farm, circus, holidays, or dinosaurs)

Mail To: Peggy's Stuff
P.O. Box 274
Avon, MA 02322-0274

PENCIL TOPPERS

PENCIL PERK-UPS

Perk up your writing utensils with these incredible **pencil toppers**—your old pencils will never be the same!

The supplier will send you two identical toppers, which will be a pair of magnifying glasses, jungle animals, bouncing woodpeckers, or waving flags.

Send: $1.00 postage & handling

Ask For: Pencil toppers

Mail To: Peggy's Stuff
P.O. Box 274
Avon, MA 02322-0274

PICTURE POSTCARDS

Snappy Snapshots

Don't waste your vacation searching for the perfect postcards to send home when you can create your own! You can turn any snapshot into an unusual personal postcard with **picture postcards.**

The set includes four sample cards and a wholesale order form. Just peel away the card's protective adhesive covering and stick it to the back of your favorite vacation photo. Presto! Your personalized postcard is ready to mail.

Send: $1.25 postage & handling

Ask For: Picture postcards

Mail To: Poster Cards
635 Milpas Street
Santa Barbara, CA 93103

A double dose of prehistoric fun, the **dinosaur pop-a-point pencil & pin set** brings everyone's favorite prehistoric creatures back to life.

DINOSAUR PENCIL & PIN SET
DYNAMITE DUO

The plastic pencil has a fantastic dinosaur design, an eraser, and a cap. The 1" button pin has a colorful picture of a lizard on it—perfect for any dinosaur lover's jacket or T-shirt.

Send: $1.00 postage & handling

Ask For: Dinosaur pop-a-point pencil & pin set

Mail To: Peggy's Stuff
P.O. Box 274
Avon, MA 02322-0274

PRETZEL PENCILS
Pliable Pencils

These fun **pretzel pencils** will bend to your every whim! The two plastic foot-long pencils can be bent and shaped into a variety of forms. Don't worry, they'll still write—no matter what shape you twist them into!

Send: $2.00 postage & handling

Ask For: Two pretzel pencils

Mail To: Mr. Rainbows
Dept. F2-42
P.O. Box 387
Avalon, NJ 08202

Rock and roll your mistakes away with these two clever **record-shaped erasers!**

Packaged in individual envelopes, the flexible 2" writing partners come in assorted colors and look just like mini record albums.

Send:	$1.00 postage & handling
Ask For:	Two record-shaped erasers
Mail To:	Peggy's Stuff
	P.O. Box 274
	Avon, MA 02322-0274

RECORD ERASERS

MUSIC FOR YOUR MISTAKES

Learn how to "say" the alphabet with your hands with this 8½" x 11" card stock **sign language alphabet poster.**

This offer also includes a fashionable, bright yellow 3" **button** of the hand positions of each letter of the alphabet. Learn this unique alphabet, and you'll be on your way to communicating with hearing-impaired people.

Send:	$2.00 postage & handling
Ask For:	Sign language alphabet poster & button
Mail To:	Keep Quiet
	P.O. Box 367
	Stanhope, NJ 07874

Here's an espionage gadget that secret agent James Bond would envy: a pair of **spy sunglasses!**

The dark plastic lenses with a rectangular black frame let you see what's going on behind you as well as keep your eyes shaded from those near you. These super specs are "for your eyes only!"

Send: $2.00 postage & handling

Ask For: Spy sunglasses

Mail To: Christian Treasures
P.O. Box 1112
Huntington Beach, CA 92647

These cute **Teddy Bear Scratch 'N Sniff stickers** are sure to spice up your life. But these bears don't just look great, they smell yummy, too—like cinnamon candy sticks!

SCENTED STICKERS
SCENT-SATIONAL STICKERS

The round decals come in six different designs on 4½" x 6" sheets. You can choose one sheet of 88 stickers or three sheets of 264 stickers.

Send: $1.00 for 88; $2.00 for 264

Ask For: Teddy Bear Scratch 'N Sniff stickers: 88 or 264

Mail To: The Very Best
Dept. TB
P.O. Box 2838
Long Beach, CA 90801-2838

EMERGENCY STICKERS

Fast Fingers

When you see an emergency, you have to be able to dial for help immediately. However, it's easy to forget the important phone numbers you need. With the **emergency phone stickers** on or near your home's phones, you'll know instantly who to call.

The offer is good for four brightly colored stickers that will help you remember exactly what your fingers need to do.

Send: $1.00 postage & handling

Ask For: Emergency phone stickers

Mail To: S. Brown
P.O. Box 568
Techny, IL 60082

Ho, Ho, Ho! These silk-screened **Christmas stickers** will add a little season's cheer to your holiday.

Each 2" square sticker has a unique design on a silver background. The 11 stickers offered include Santa Claus, a Christmas tree, a gingerbread man, and many more. Stick them on cards or wrapping paper and enjoy the merry season.

CHRISTMAS STICKERS

'TIS THE SEASON

Send: $1.00 postage & handling

Ask For: Christmas stickers

Mail To: Expressions
Dept. CFB
1668 Valtec Lane
Boulder, CO 80301

To beat the homework blues, send for a pair of friendly **bookworm pencils.**

Each standard No. 2 pencil comes with a fuzzy worm with bulging eyes and a round snout. The pencils come in an assortment of colors. Writing has never been so fun!

BOOKWORM PENCILS

Nutty Note-Takers

Send:	$1.00 for one; $1.75 for two
Ask For:	Bookworm pencils
Mail To:	G. C. Hebbe P.O. Box 337 Lanoka Harbor, NJ 08734

METALLIC STICKERS

STICK IT TO THEM!

Whether for a class project, a notebook cover, or a spiral binder, these **metallic stickers** are sure to liven up any school subject.

You will receive three sheets of heart, duck, and dinosaur stickers. Start your collection today!

Send:	$1.50 postage & handling
Ask For:	Three sheets of stickers
Mail To:	Eccor Wholesale 3710 Mendenhall S. Memphis, TN 38115

Note your hopes for our planet or your wishes for conservation in your school and your neighborhood; write away for this **Earth Friends stationery set** and convey your thoughts to a friend.

The set includes four white envelopes and six sheets of 5½" x 8½" light green paper printed with the Earth Friends logo.

Send: $2.00 postage & handling

Ask For: Earth Friends stationery set

Mail To: United Earth Friends®
P.O. Box 51106
Raleigh, NC 27609

Protect your right to breathe clean air! Send for this **no-smoking sign** that says, "Lungs at Work, No Smoking."

> *NO-SMOKING SIGN*
> # STOP IN THE NAME OF HEALTH

Produced by the American Lung Association, this friendly red-and-white reminder is shaped like a stop sign. Smokers will have to think twice about lighting up in your home when they see this sign.

Send: Your name & address

Ask For: No-smoking sign

Mail To: American Lung Association
P.O. Box 596-FB, #0121
New York, NY 10116-0596

STICKERS

Global Gusto

This set of 20 **EarthSeals stickers** will remind you to take care of our environment.

Each 2" round sticker shows a colorful NASA photograph of Earth taken from outer space.

Send: A long SASE plus $2.00 postage & handling

Ask For: EarthSeals stickers

Mail To: EarthSeals
P.O. Box 8000-FBW
Berkeley, CA 94707

FREE   FREE   FREE

Something for nothing!! Hundreds of dollars' worth of items are listed in each issue of *FREEBIES Magazine*. Five times a year each issue features at least 100 FREE and low-postage-&-handling-only offers, including fun toys, great magazines, and awesome craft ideas.

Have you purchased a "Free Things" book before—only to find that the items were unavailable? That won't happen with FREEBIES—all of our offers are verified for accuracy with the suppliers!

☑   Yes—Send me 5 issues for only $5.00 (save 60% off the cover price)

☐   Payment Enclosed, or Charge   ☐ VISA   ☐ MasterCard

Card Number _ _ _ _ _ _ _ _ _ _ _ _ _ _ _ _   Exp. Date _ _/_ _

Name_____

Address_____

City _____ State_____ Zip_____

Daytime Phone (_ _ _) _ _ _ – _ _ _ _
(in case we have a question about your subscription)

Send to: *FREEBIES Magazine*
           1135 Eugenia Place, Carpinteria, CA 93013